D like DOLL
E like
EVIL

READER REVIEWS

"An awesome page turner! Mr. Olfet is among the rising top writers of this generation."

- Kyle Davis

D like DOLL E like EVIL

Omid Olfet

READERSMAGNET, LLC

D Like Doll E Like Evil
Copyright © 2017 by Omid Olfet.

Published in the United States of America
ISBN Paperback: 978-1-947765-04-7
ISBN eBook: 978-1-947765-05-4

All rights reserved. No part of this publication may be reproduced, stored in a retrieval system or transmitted in any way by any means, electronic, mechanical, photocopy, recording or otherwise without the prior permission of the author except as provided by USA copyright law.

No lines, parts and quotations was taken from other books or any previous publications. The opinions expressed by the author are not necessarily those of ReadersMagnet, LLC.

ReadersMagnet, LLC
80 Broad Street, 5th & 6th Floors Finance District | New York City, NY 10004 USA
1.646. 880. 9760 | www.readersmagnet.com

Book design copyright © 2017 by ReadersMagnet, LLC. All rights reserved.
Cover design by Ericka Walker
Interior design by Shieldon Watson

Child abuse is still one of the major problems in some countries. As it follows John is one of the many victims in the world. His parents were married in 1969. After the first week of marriage, John's parents separated from each other and they started a new life. In that situation, John was the only problem that his parents had. John's dad was willing to persuade his ex-wife to abort the child, but his ex-wife didn't want that to happen because she loved her baby. Mary was a mother in a real sense of the word, which is why she wanted to prevent the abortion from happening at any cost. John's dad - Max was a very strict and for the lack of better words, a dictator. It was like he had no passion towards his unborn child. Max was trying to use his mother as a mediator to convince his ex-wife to abort the child. "I never liked her from the very beginning, why should we keep the baby then?" Max told his mother, "This is a sin; did you know that?" Max's mother told his son: "He is a gift from God to you and aborting the child is a sin." Max's mother continued, "Mom listen to me, there is no sense to it. His life is going to be ruined and we cannot make him happy. Think about it!" Max said. "You shouldn't have done that from the very beginning and now it's too late, son." Max's mother said. "Please don't do it, please we are going to be cursed." Max's mother said while wiping her tears off her face. As a matter of fact, Max was raised in a very religious family. That's why the word cursed shocked him a little bit and he changed his mind. "Ok Mom, ok we're not going to do it. Are you happy now?" Max told his mom in an unhappy way. "Thank you, my son, God blesses your heart." Max's mom said while stretching her arms to hug her son. "He is a boy and he is going to be very sweet." Max's mother said. "He is going to bring you luck in your life." Max's mother continued. "I can tell from the very beginning." Max said sarcastically. "Everything is God's will; never forget that." Max's mother named Martha said. This was a big decision for the Max family and it turned the page of their lives into a different phase. Mary, who got very excited about the decision to keep the baby, hugged her ex-husband and kissed him a lot.

It was August 1970, the time of happiness and excitement for Mary and the grandma Martha and the father of Max, since John was born. At the time of birth, almost everyone was in the hospital. He is a big boy, one of the doctors told Mary. "What name did you choose for him?" a nurse asked. "John!" Mary responded. "A beautiful name." the nurse said, "God bless you all." she continued. "Thanks for everything doctor." Mary said. "No problem at all." the doctor said and he went away. The judge had decided to give the responsibility of taking care of the baby to the father. That is why the sadness was not fading out from the mother's face. She wanted to breastfeed the baby, but with the Judge's decision, she had a hard time doing that. John was about to face a hard life, and there was no way for him to change his destiny. The judge's decision was based on the parent's income and since Mary was just a housewife, she didn't qualify in taking care of her son. Max was raised in a very rich family and by the time he was a very rich businessman. So financially he was even more than qualified to be the child's guardian, but things don't go well all the time. The same thing goes for the sky which is not clear every day.

Soon the quietness before the storm changed and the blue sky turned black-A step mom. Remember that they say a married couple should come in white and go in white. Martha told Max "Please don't make the same mistake again?" "No mom, this time it's different, I love her from the bottom of my heart." Max said. "I hope so and I'll pray for you." Martha said. "You are my only son and I don't want to see you alone." Martha continued and hugged her son. Max was so excited to have fallen in love with an older lady than him, named Sara. Sara came from a poor family, and the only advantage she had was her beauty. Imagine a lady with lower than average income and low education, with a beautiful face, a combination of beauty and beast. Snake's skin is beautiful as well, but the question is if beauty is everything or not. Anyways, time was going to answer the question and everything started with a majestic ceremony. Playing music, singing songs, and dancing was a good start with serving delicious foods, drinks, and deserts. Two love birds were connected. One of them was a fooled one and the other one turned evil. It was a fabulous ceremony indeed and John was 1-year old at the time.

A stranger came to John's life, which had no passion towards him. That made sense because John was not from her blood. There are some exceptions of course but this one was not the one. Sara was a blond with blue eyes and John got the blues. The 1-year old John still felt depression and sadness. Did Sara seduce Max? This was a good question that nobody knew the answer, besides them. Time clears so many things including honesty. In about a year after their marriage, Max found out that Sara's parents bought them a very big house. The house seemed to be one of the very expensive ones, maybe more than a million dollars. Max got really astonished. "Where did they get that much money?" Max asked himself, as the whole thing was very surprising. Perhaps they must have won a lottery ticket or something, Max thought to himself. On the other hand, Max who was very busy with his business didn't even have enough time to spend with his family. Therefore, he decided to put John with his mom, Martha. Max knew that his mother loved his grandson very much and he was sure she would take good care of the baby. When Max consulted that with his mother, Martha got so excited that she burst to tears. "It is not going to be a long time." Max told his mother. "As soon as the business gets a little slow I am going to pick him up." Max continued. "He can stay here with us as long as you want him to." Martha said. "I'll pray for you." Max told his mom, putting a $1000 check in her hand and he thanked her a lot and said bye to his mom. Max hugged his son and kissed him once again before he left them. A little smile appeared in John's face since he loved his grandma, but at the same time he didn't like seeing his dad going away and he was going to miss him.

Max returned to his hometown to take care of his business. "I'm going to miss him." Max told Sara. Sara acted like a smart politician and said "Everything is going to be okay. He is going to enjoy his time with his grandma and soon you are going to see him again." Sara continued. "Indeed!" Sara was so excited about that. She hated John from the bottom of her heart. Now that John was not with them it was a perfect time for her to relax and enjoy her time. "I'm going to miss him too!" Sara told Max pretending. That was really a big lie. Most step moms don't like their step children, but sometimes it is smart to act like a politician. Sara promised to take care of John before marriage otherwise the marriage even wouldn't have happened. Sara's life was full on lies and dishonesty.

The fluctuation in the market is a normal thing. Sometimes the business is slow and sometimes it is busy. Sometimes the economy is so slow for a longtime, which we call recession. Max business was not an exception. The problem is that you cannot tell how long the recession is going to last. In Max's case, it lasted a long time. The problem started with the stocks. Max had bought so many stocks from different companies in the past. Max was a type of person having good experiences with buying stocks in the past. He was an intelligent man, knowing when to buy and what to buy. But one cannot always be lucky, if luck is the right word to use. So many people believed in luck whereas a good amount doesn't. Unfortunately, in the recession time, all the stocks Max had bought before dropped very severely and they did not go up any more. The stocks that Max had the most shares belonged to an oil company. Due to the number of stocks Max had bought before, he lost a lot of money. A lot, hundreds of thousands of dollars! Max was facing two choices; one of them was selling the stocks at a very low price. The other one was waiting for the economy to get better. Since Max didn't have enough backup money for the second option, he had to choose the first one. This means announcing bankruptcy. This was the point where Max's life had changed to a complete different phase. Max's life turned upside down, but on the contrary Sara's parents became rich.

One day in a family reunion something grabbed Max's attention. A portrait is something that he had lost a long time ago. Max was an artist, not like the regular artists that you can see everywhere- a very professional one. When he was a kid, Martha sent him to an art class. As a matter of fact, he didn't care about being famous. He cared about doing a job just for the love of it. One day that goes back to a long time ago; Max asked his teacher if he could do him a favor. "What is that?" The teacher asked. "Since love is the most important thing in the world, would you be able to show it in a picture for me?" Max asked his teacher. "You are asking me a hard question." the teacher responded. "Indeed! This is too hard for me; as a matter of fact it is almost impossible." "At least you can give it a try, can't you?" Max asked. "I'm afraid of something." Max's teacher said. "What is that?" Max responded. "I'm afraid it wouldn't show a real picture of love." Max's teacher responded. "Please, at least give it a try and do your best." Max told his teacher. "Why are you insisting so much?" The teacher asked. Max who loved his teacher a lot answered "Because, I love you" without even thinking about the question. "I want to know what it looks like." Max continued. "Okay, but don't expect me to be perfect." Max's teacher said. "No, I am not in a rush, I just want to see." Max said. It took a while before Max could realize something out of the picture. The brush was moving on the board and Max could hardly wait for the result. After two hours working hard, a mother's face appeared on the board looking at her child's face so passionately. Max jumped and grabbed the portrait with both hands and kissed the picture so fast that he didn't even realize that the picture was still wet. "Hey, look at you!" Max's teacher said while laughing. It took Max a few seconds before realizing what had happened. The board was covering Max's face while holding the board in his hands. Max moved the picture away from his face to see why his teacher was laughing at him. The teacher was still laughing very sweetly pointing his index finger to Max's face, "What had happened?" Max still didn't know until he realized in a few seconds that something wrong had happened to his face. So far it was a guess, until he took another quick look at the picture and saw his lip mark on the picture. He couldn't wipe it off because he was still holding the picture in his hands. Max put the picture in its place and he was still kind of shocked for seconds. It was like he didn't even know what to do first. Should he apologize, laugh, or wipe his face. Finally, he decided to apologize, "Sorry. I'm very sorry." Max said. By the time the teacher had stopped laughing and he was smiling instead. "Now, there's a signature on my piece of Art." the teacher said. At the time Max didn't realize what his teacher meant by that, but he figured it out long time after. "Even if my job wasn't perfect, you made it perfectly complete." Max's teacher said. "Can I have it like that?" Max asked his teacher. "I don't want to bother you with redoing it." Max continued. "Sure, accept this as a gift from your teacher." Max's teacher responded.

Right before the family reunion, Sara's parents asked Max if he could help them with moving into their new house. It was a back breaking job. "Okay, would you take this side please?" Sara's dad told Max, showing the edge of their refrigerator, which was facing the wall.

Max pushed the refrigerator a little bit to be able to move behind it. The refrigerator was pushed enough for a portrait hiding behind it to fall. As soon as the portrait fell on the kitchen floor, Max grabbed it to put it somewhere else. As soon as Max saw the portrait he got shocked. Yes, it was his, and there was absolutely no way for a duplicate to exist. Max took a quick look at the picture before putting it somewhere else. Everything looked like the exact same picture he used to have, but what was it doing there. The lip marks were still there and that was proof that the picture was his, but who brought it there. That is the question Max wanted to find the answer to. Max had the picture before getting married to Sara; so, he should have investigated the case accordingly. After they moved the refrigerator to the truck; Max talked to Sara's father about the picture. "I found a picture behind your refrigerator, did you notice that?" Max asked. "Oh really, where is it?" Sara's father replied. Max went to the picture and grabbed it to show it to Sara's dad. "It is a beautiful piece of art, isn't it?" Max asked Sara's dad, who was surprised and one could tell that from his face he was in awe. "He said that it is a master piece; I had never seen this before." he continued. "Why did you put it behind the refrigerator?" Max asked. "It is a beautiful picture; you should have put it on the wall." Max continued. "Yes, I know!" Sara's father replied. "This is the first time I've seen this picture, I don't even know who put it. I should ask my wife." Sara's father continued. From then on Max got suspicious of his wife and her parents. This was the beginning of so many arguments between Max and his wife. As a matter of fact, Max was looking for any kind of excuse to start the argument, because there was no more trust between Max and his wife.

Max still loved his son who was still with his grandma. John who was 2 years old now, was a very bright and talented boy. His IQ was much higher than average. Mary visited her son occasionally. By the time Mary had married to an older man; her husband was about 10 years older than her. Mary's husband had his own ranch and that was the way he made a living. Of course, his job was kind of hard for a man of his age.

One day, Mary decided to buy a toy for John before visiting him. She had missed her son a lot, because it was a long time that she hadn't seen him. She was walking by the stores when she saw a toy shop. Some of the beautiful toys were being shown up by the window. These included car toys of all kinds and some toys which were movie characters. Some of the toys were war toys such as helicopters, bombers, and tanks. Among the toys behind the window there was a section for girls too. Some of these were female characters in movies and dolls. There was a doll among all of them which was totally different. There was a magic in the doll's eyes. As soon as Mary saw the doll she stopped looking at the other toys, as if she was kind of hypnotized. The influential power in the doll's eyes was beyond imagination. The eyes were like strong magnets which could absorb anything onto them. Mary looked and looked and looked. Better to say she was staring at the doll's face. "Is there anything that I can help you with ma'am?" The salesman who was standing by the entry door asked. As a matter of fact, the salesman was watching Mary for quite a while, but Mary didn't even notice. "No, I was just looking." Mary who was shocked responded brokenly. "Beautiful toys aren't they?" the salesman asked. "Oh yes, they are gorgeous." Mary answered. "Take your time ma'am, just let me know if you need any help." the salesman said. "Sure, I will thank you." Mary responded. "No problem at all." the salesman said and went inside. Mary took another quick look at the doll as if she was trying not to let the doll capture her soul, but it was too late she had already fallen in love with the doll. She made a firm decision and stepped inside with a little smile on her face. "Yes ma'am, are you ready?" the sales man asked. "I guess I am." Mary responded. "How much is the doll there?" Mary asked, pointing to the doll. "Which one?" the salesman asked stepping forward towards Mary. "That doll sitting on that shelf!" Mary said showing the doll to the sales man. The salesman looked at the doll and said "Oh that's the gorgeous one." "Yes, it is." Mary said. "How much is it?" Mary asked again. "That is one of a kind; you cannot find it anywhere else besides this store." the salesman said. "Let me tell you a little bit about the doll before I tell you the price; is that okay with you?" the salesman said. Mary then replied with yes go ahead. "The doll is an antique; its history goes back to 1500. The first owner of the doll was a witch." the salesman said. "A witch?" Mary who didn't expect to hear such a thing asked in a surprised tone. "Yes, you heard it right." the salesman replied. Mary who didn't believe in those things said "Okay, I'm in a hurry, would you please tell me the price? I've got to go." "Sure, but if you need more information about the doll read the little booklet that comes with It." the salesman said. "The doll is $200." Mary who was shocked asked if it was made out of gold or something while raising her voice. "Ma'am, there is no reason to be surprised, I was going to give you more information about the doll, but you were in a rush." the sales man said. "There is no way I'm going to pay $200 for a doll!" Mary said while she was about to step out of the door disappointed. "Ma'am wait!" the salesman said. "Since this is the last item and we have had it for a long time and nobody has bought it, I can give you a discount of 20%. This is the lowest price ($160) I can sell it to you!" the sales man continued. "It is still too expensive." Mary said.

"Well that's it, I cannot give it to you any cheaper." the salesman said with a determined tone. Mary got kind of upset and said "No thank you I'm not going to pay that much for a doll, you have a good evening." Mary stepped out of the store. "Remember it is a special doll." the salesman said loudly while Mary was getting far. Mary didn't even turn her back and she kept going.

Mary was not very far from the store when a voice called to her and asked, isn't your son special to you? Mary who was shocked stopped for a second; maybe it was her imagination, she thought to herself. When she started to walk again the voice stopped her and said "Your son is worth more than $160 to you, isn't he? "Who are you?" Mary asked, nobody answered. "I guess I'm going crazy." Mary told herself. "You are not crazy, but what you did is crazy." the voice talked to her again. "So, you think I should have paid $160 for a doll? As a matter of fact, this is crazy." "Mary talked to herself. You should have bought a special gift for a special person, don't you think so?" The voice asked. "What is so special about it?" Mary asked. "You are going to figure it out later." the voice responded. "Okay, okay I'm tired of you I'm going to buy it for my son." Mary said. "Good! You are not going to be sorry for that." the voice said.

Mary returned to the store, they were about to close. Yes, ma'am did you change your mind? The salesman asked while holding a lock in his hand. "I guess everything is going against my will", Mary said. "Why can you say so?" The salesman asked. "Just give it to me I don't want to talk about it anymore", Mary said impatiently. "As you wish", the sales man said while pulling the doll out of the case. "Come out my girl." the salesman said as if he was talking to a real person. "Be a good girl so your mama wouldn't get mad at you", the salesman was still talking. Mary was ready to pay. Okay, $160+Tax came up to $170. "Great can't be better than that", Mary said sarcastically and she paid for the doll with a frown on her face. "I'm telling you it's worth it", the salesman said. "You are not going to be sorry for buying that", the salesman continued while he was handing the doll to Mary. "Thank you", Mary said unhappily and she stepped out of the store, "By the way I forgot to tell you that she talks a little bit too." The salesman said loudly. "Whatever", Mary responded loudly and she got far from the store. By the time Mary got home she was tired and she went straight to bed.

The next day when she opened her eyes the first thing that came to her mind was her son and the gift she was going to give him. With this thought she got so excited that the remaining sleepiness went away from her eyes. The excitement gave so much energy to Mary that it made her jump in the bed to go to the doll. As soon as she reached the doll, she grabbed it like a mother holding her baby in her arms. Zorostes, Zorostes, Zorostes three times. Mary didn't know what the word meant; so she decided to go back to the book shelf to find the meaning in the dictionary. She turned the pages over and over under the letter Z. She was so excited, but unfortunately, she couldn't find any meaning to the mentioned word. Then she went to the computer in the hope of finding a definition for the word. She typed the word and pressed the enter key. "We did not find results for Zorostes" The computer said. Mary got very disappointed and kind of upset. She went to the phone and called the toy store. "Good morning this is a toy store, can I help you?" Somebody answered. "Good morning sir, this is Mary, I bought a doll from you guys last night, you remember?" Mary asked. "Yes, how you are doing mam", the man responded. "I'm doing fine", Mary said. "Something is confusing me, this morning when I touched the doll, it talked to me", Mary continued. "Oh really, I told you ma'am that the doll talks", the salesman said. "Now tell me what it said", the salesman asked. "The doll said Zorostes", Mary replied. "I searched it up in my dictionary and my computer. There was no definition for it", Mary continued. "Yes, ma'am you are right that's the only word the doll says and nobody has found a pattern for it." The salesman said. "Nobody knows under what circumstances the doll might talk and don't bother yourself with finding the definition for it, because in more than 500 years nobody has figured it out", the salesman continued. "Sometimes it can be annoying", Mary said. "You know what the solution is, it's very simple, anytime you think it bothers you, get a screw driver and open the small battery panel. This should be located on the back of the doll. Then get the batteries out of the place", the salesman said. "In order to do that you need to take her clothes off; I guess I didn't even need to tell you that, right?" The sales man asked. "Right", Mary answered. "I need to let you know about something else", the salesman said. "What is that?" Mary answered. "There is one guess about what the doll says and I repeat it is just a guess. It may be a spell but a passive one since it doesn't do anything", the sales man said. "As I said the owner of the doll was a witch and you can read the rest of the story in the booklet". "Is there anything else I should know about the doll?" Mary asked. "I guess that is it", the sales man answered. "If you have any more questions I would be more than glad to answer", the sales man continued. "Thank you, sir", Mary said and hung up the phone. It was like she was still thinking about something.

Mary went to the closet where she had put the doll box very quickly. She opened the door and grabbed the box and dug in there for the booklet, without looking inside the box. As soon as she realized she was touching something, she grabbed it out of the box. Yes, it was a package having a booklet and a sheet of paper showing the instructions for using the doll. Mary opened the package very curiously and she got the booklet out of the package.

The front cover of the booklet was saying **"A doll which belonged to a witch"** and then there was a date showing below that **"1435-1486"**. Mary looked at the front cover for a little while and then she opened the booklet cautiously. The first page was a blank page. Mary turned the page and she saw the title of the book with the date below again. Since there was nothing else on that page, Mary turned the page again. It was the table of contents, starting with **"The life of a witch"** and the page numbers. Then on the second line it was showing **"The Death of a Witch"** with the page numbers. On the third line, which was the last line on the contents page, it was showing **"A Doll Which Belonged to a Witch"**. Although Mary really wanted to start right off the last part, but for some reason she started from the very beginning. Mary turned the content page and started reading the booklet eagerly. **"The Life of a Witch"** *A girl was born in a very poor family in 1435. Unfortunately there is no record of her name in the history. She was a very beautiful girl, as beautiful as an angel. As she grew up all other girls around were jealous of her.*

Her family was too poor to send her to school; that's why her parents made her help around the house. The beautiful girl was not able to appear in a nice and beautiful dress, because obviously her parents didn't have enough money to spend on her. Her parents were truly God believers, but the girl diverted away from her parent's path. She always watched her parents praying to God, and she found that in contradiction to her parent's financial situation. She always thought to herself, if there was such a thing as God why wouldn't he answer her parent's prayers. That was a beginning of a tragic change in her destiny.

One day the beautiful girl found a doll on her way back home. The doll had a beautiful face, but at that moment it looked so ugly because her face was covered with mud and so was her clothes. The beautiful girl grabbed the doll as if she found some treasure. Of course her parents were hardly able to feed her, so how would they be able to buy her any toys. The doll was her first toy, that's why the beautiful girl was so excited to have found the doll. She hugged the doll instantly with so much passion, without even being aware of the mud on the doll's clothes. She said some words to the doll, as if the doll could understand what she was saying. While she was doing all that, a pedestrian was watching her or better to say, was spying on her. The pedestrian waited till the girl decided to go back home with the doll in her hands. The man chased after the girl until she went inside the house and shut the door.

Mama, look what I found, the girl said. Her mother who was working in the kitchen said I'm here in the kitchen, what did you find? Her mother asked. By the time the girl was in the kitchen behind her mother. Close your eyes and turn back, the girl told her mom, don't open your eyes until I tell you. Okay, okay! The mother said impatiently and she followed the order. Okay, now you can open, the girl who was so excited told her mother. Her mother opened her eyes and found a doll in her daughter's hands. Isn't that beautiful? The girl asked her mother. Wow it's gorgeous, where did you find it? Her mother asked. I found it out there in the mud close to our house, the girl answered. Oh my sweet heart it's so beautiful. Don't worry about the mud, because it rained last night, her mother said. It is not a big deal at all, we can wash off her face and clothes, her mother continued. Can you really do that for me? The girl asked. Of course, we can, why not, her mother replied.

In the meanwhile, that they were talking about the doll, somebody knocked on the door. Okay sweetie I'll be right back, her mother said and she rushed towards the door. Who is it? Mother asked. Nobody answered. Who is it? Mother asked again. Nobody answered this time either. She carefully opened the door. It was the pedestrian with a grin on his face. May I speak to the head of the house? The pedestrian asked. He is not here now; can I take a message? The mother asked. Well I guess I can talk to you, can't I? The pedestrian asked. Sure why not, the mother replied. Come on in and have a seat, the mother said and she shut the door. Well I don't know how to start, but it is about your daughter, the pedestrian said. What about her? What happened? The mother asked anxiously. Well nothing to worry about if you take it seriously now, the pedestrian replied. What is that? Tell me, the mother said. I'm afraid to tell you there is something wrong with your daughter, the pedestrian said. What? What is it? The mother asked. I saw her talking to a doll using unfamiliar words, the pedestrian said. Do you remember what kind of words? The mother asked. Unfortunately I didn't understand even a single word of what she was talking about, the pedestrian said. Well that's strange the mother said. No offense, are you sure your daughter is in a normal mental condition? The pedestrian asked. Yes of course, what do you mean? The mother asked angrily. I was just going to make sure, the pedestrian replied. Just be careful about her, the pedestrian continued. Sure, the mother said. The pedestrian stood up and walked towards the entry door. You have a nice day, the pedestrian said. You as well, the mother said and she shut the door.

The mother went back to the kitchen, but she couldn't find her daughter there. She called her a few times, I'm right here behind you, were you looking for me? The girl said. The mother got shocked and scared a little bit. Oh my god you scared me, the mother said. I'm sorry, but I was here. The girl said. Are you going to wash my doll? The girl *asked. Yes, I'm going to do it for you now, the mother said with a little delay. Is it possible to change her clothes too? The girl asked. Well I'll think about it, the mother said. I should look for some fabrics, the mother continued. Oh, I figure out I can use your small size clothes, because they don't fit you anymore, the mother added. It's wonderful, you mean my baby clothes, right? The girl asked. Right you are so smart my love, the mother replied.*

Everything went by very smoothly until her father heard some weird stuff about her daughter from the people in town. Have you heard about what the people say about your daughter? A friend asked the father. No, what do they say? The father asked. All sorts of stuff, some people say your daughter is crazy and that she has lost her mind. Other said your daughter talks to herself, and I heard some people talk about her doll. As soon as the father heard those things, he lost his control and got really mad and raised his voice very angrily. Who said these things about my daughter? The father asked in a defending manner. Alright now, take it easy man. So many people talk about your daughter nowadays. The friend said. There are so many of them what can you do about them? The friend asked. The father tried to control himself after he heard that. First you should know why they are saying those things about your daughter. The friend said. You can't stop them if you don't know the reason. You know what I'm talking about, right? The friend asked. Yes, I do, the father replied. Don't get mad at me for being honest with you. I've heard things about your daughter even worse than that, the friend said. What things? The father asked. First promise me that you won't get mad, the friend said. Okay I promise, the father said impatiently. The people say your daughter is a witch, the friend said. The people say my daughter is a what? The father asked very angrily. As a matter of fact as soon as he heard that word, his face became scarily red, due to extreme anger. Who said that, you just tell me the names I'm going to kill them, the father said. Okay man calm down, remember you promised, the friend said. As I said you should find the reason before jumping to conclusions, the friend continued. How would I know the reason? The father asked. Well I heard things about your daughter's doll as I said before, the friend said. I guess that can help you a lot, the friend continued. What have you heard about the doll? The father asked. I heard your daughter has a beautiful doll. Is that right? The friend asked. Yes, but what does this situation have to do with a doll, the father asked. Be patient and I'll tell you, the friend said. I heard she loves the doll and she shows so much passion towards it. Am I correct? The friend asked. Correct and I heard sometimes she talks to the doll, right? The friend asked. Right, the father replied. Well, that's it. We should know more about the doll, the friend said. The father who didn't understand anything from what his friend told him, said are you out of your mind? That's just a doll and my girl likes it, the father continued. Well, I guess *the problem is far beyond that, the friend said. You should spy on your daughter, I'm not crazy, the friend continued. You know what, I take that as an insult to my daughter and me, the father said. As you wish, but remember you cannot shut people's mouths, if you don't do what I just told you, the friend said. Trust me, I'm your friend, the friend continued and then said bye. The father went into deep thought that he even forgot to say goodbye back to his friend.*

The day father went home he looked at everybody very strangely. What's the matter darling? His wife asked. Oh what? Nothing's wrong. The father answered. I know there is something, you know that you can't hide it from me right? His wife said stretching her arms to hug her husband with a sweet smile on her face. You've never been like that, his wife added. Well I'm just tired, the father said pretending. You want a drink or something? His wife asked. Yes, if you don't mind, the father replied. He asked about his daughter while his wife was going to grab a cup of water for him. She was here just a minute ago, the mother said and then she called to her. But they didn't hear an answer. That's strange, the mother said. She was playing with her doll just before you came, the mother continued. You know what, the father asked with a delay. What? The mother asked. That doll is causing trouble, the father said. Why? What happened? The mother asked. So many things happened, the father replied. Like what? The mother asked. That doll is ruining our reputation, did you know that? The father asked. No why, can you explain what has happened. The mother said. No I don't have time now, I'll tell you later, the father said. The first thing we should do is find that doll. The father said and he hurried outside. The mother called to him although it was useless.

There is a lapse in the history of the life of a witch at this point. The death of a witch: *There is a record of the beautiful girl who grew up with a bad reputation. Her life was sad and full of sorrow. Her parents started hating her since she didn't tell them about the doll and where she was hiding her. She was so scared of losing her only toy and then in return she lost her parent's love; because as mentioned before her parents didn't want to lose their good reputation just for a stupid doll. Although they loved their daughter so much, in other words they didn't want to sell their reputation for the price of keeping the doll. Spying on the girl appeared to be entirely useless, because anytime the parents went for spying for some reason; they didn't get any positive results. As if the girl knew everything. Was she using her sixth sense? Or she knew about telepathic communication? Or maybe she really was a witch. Nobody had the answers to these questions. What did that have to do with the doll? Only she knew.*

One day the parents found their daughter's picture on the newspaper. Headlines were **"A Witch against God".** *The paper was talking about a big reward to be given to whoever finds the girl and gives information about her to* *the authorities. Everybody in the town was showing the girl's picture to each other. Of course everybody was after the prize. On one hand the parents were so sad because naturally they loved their daughter, but on the other hand they loved God too and they didn't want such a thing to distract them from paying attention to their religious beliefs. Tears dropped off the mother's eyes and she knelt down to pray for her daughter. You could see the sign of deep sadness on the father's face too. The girl's picture on the paper could be a sign of big trouble for the girl. What were they going to do to the girl? This was the question the people were asking each other. Maybe her life was in big danger.*

During a very cold winter they found her in an herb shop buying some herbs for her cough. She was coughing badly and she was not even aware of her picture in the newspaper. Do you have something for cough sir, the girl said. Yes of course the salesman said, while he was going to get the herb off the shelf. Here you are, the salesman said giving the flask of herb to the girl, and he took a quick look at her face. As soon as he saw the girl he remembered the picture in the paper. What should I do with it? The girl asked. Empty the whole flask in water and boil it for 5 minutes and it's ready to drink, the salesman said. This time he looked at the girl's face longer than the first time. The girl paid for the herbal medicine and she started coughing really badly, while she was trying to say goodbye to the salesman. You have a nice day ma'am, the salesman said. While doing this, he used one hand for waving at her and the other one for summoning the constable who then contacted the local police units. In a little while the police found her not too far from the store while she was still coughing, covering her mouth with one hand, and holding something in her other hand- the doll.

The investigations took a long time. The girl was not as young as before, as a matter of fact she had some wrinkles on her face. She was not as strong as before either, because she was shaking a little bit. Plus all of that, she was not in a good health condition. What do you want from me? The girl asked the cops brokenly. You have to come with us, the cops replied. Come to where? The girl asked. You'll know later, the cops replied. I haven't done anything wrong, the girl said. She was right; she had an innocent face and a beautiful heart, as nice as an angel. Unfortunately the cops and the people didn't care about that.

When they reached the police station the cops passed her through a corridor, before entering a room. There were more investigations coming. There was a guy sitting in a chair dressed in normal clothes, maybe he was undercover. Okay ma'am, tell us about the doll. Where did you get that doll from? The man asked. The girl who didn't know what to say at first, said I found it a long time ago when I was a little kid. You are a liar, the man shouted and tapped on his desk very hard. That's not true, I've never lied in my life, the girl said in a defending manner while she was shaking due to extreme anger. Don't raise your voice here, the man said sarcastically. We will show it to you, we have a witness. How about that? The man asked. That is not right, your witness is a liar too, the girl said. I guess you think everybody is a liar but you right? The man asked. I didn't say everybody is a liar, but what you are talking about is a big lie, the girl said and started coughing very badly. By the way what were you doing inside the herb shop? The investigator asked. I was riding a bicycle, the girl replied sarcastically. I guess you are intentionally trying to make me mad. Did you pay for the medicine or you stole it like the doll? The man asked. I have never stolen anything from anybody, understand? The girl said. Oh understood, you went to the herb shop because you were sick, by the way you are always sick. As a matter of fact, you are mentally sick, the man said. That's not true, if somebody is sick that's nobody but you, the girl said very angrily.

At this time somebody knocked on the door. Come on in, the investigator said. Two people came in the room. One of them was an officer in uniform, the other one was in a regular outfit. Here is the witness sir, the officer said. Thank you, the investigator replied. You can go, the investigator continued. The officer left and the man in normal dress attire stayed. So you denied stealing the doll, is that right, the investigator asked the girl. Yes, and I still do, the girl replied. Well, you know that nobody is going to listen to you right, because we have a witness, the investigator said. I don't care because I didn't do it, the girl said. Oh really, you are a very stubborn girl, the investigator said. I don't care what you think, but you'd better know the law is going to punish you, the investigator replied. The girl remained silent at this time. Now, tell us about yourself and what you saw years ago, the investigator asked the witness. The witness introduced himself and began to talk. I know she is a witch. I was there while she was talking to her doll and the doll talked back to her, the witness said. I'm positive that she knows about spells, the witness continued. Okay that's enough, the investigator said. Did you hear what he just said? The investigator asked the girl. The girl remained silent again. To be silent is not going to help you in court, you know that right? The investigator said in a relaxed tone. Now can you pass the doll to me? The investigator asked. The girl remained silent again and didn't show any reaction. Now you see, I told you, she doesn't even want to be separated from the doll for seconds, the witness said. Where did you say she stole the doll from again? The investigator asked. She stole it from a random pedestrian, the witness replied slowly trying to make up the story. At this time the investigator stood up hastily and rushed towards the girl very angrily. He wanted to grab the doll from the girl's hands by force. The girl was holding the doll tightly, but the investigator overcame and he got the doll out of her hands. The girl burst to tears and she shouted give the doll back to me, while she was crying. She said this so loudly that it was hard to recognize what she was saying. As I said, this is not *yours, the investigator said very rudely. It doesn't belong to you in the first place, the investigator continued. Do you understand what belonging means? The investigator asked sarcastically. Finders' keepers, the girl shouted louder this time. The investigator was looking at the doll and inspecting it carefully without paying attention. It was as if he could not even hear what the girl was talking about. Indeed, it is a beautiful doll, the investigator talked to himself. No wonder girls fall in love with it, the investigator talked to himself a little louder. Here you are to take a look at it, make sure it is the same doll. The investigator told the witness while he was giving the doll to him. The girl had already stopped crying. Yes, I have no doubt, the witness said. This is the exact same doll I saw years ago, I can still remember, the witness continued. Okay we're done, be ready for the court date, the investigator told the girl.*

The judgment system in those times was by no way fair. They didn't even give the right of having a lawyer to the girl. The girl spent her remaining days in jail. They treated the girl very badly. They tortured her a lot. These methods included sleep, food, and water deprivation, and physical punishments. Worse than all those punishments to her was taking the doll away from her. This shows how much she cared about her doll, or better to say how much she loved it. Without the doll she wanted to die rather than live. As if she didn't care about other torments. Every day she was thinking about the doll. I hope they don't throw it away, she thought to herself. They say normally, little girls care about dolls, not grown-ups. It was different in this case. What kind of attachment and connection was there between the girl and the doll? Nobody knew, except for the girl.

The court time arrived. So many people attended the session, many of them were curious about what was going to happen to the girl. The judge ordered for silence. The audience was still making a little noise, some were whispering. The judge ordered for silence again. The judge asked the witness to stand up. After the formal procedure such as taking oath and other things, the judge asked the witness to introduce himself and tell the audience about what he witnessed. The witness did as he was ordered to. Everybody was listening carefully. When the witness finished, the judge ordered him to take a seat. Then it was the girl's turn to speak. The girl started talking about her miserable life from the very beginning to the present. She really wanted to impress the audience, in the hope of convincing the judge that she was innocent. Since she had a very good memory, she barely missed anything. That's why it took her quite a long time to finish with her story. It was like the audiences were a bunch of heartless people, since only a few of them were impressed with the girl's life. The court room began to become noisy again. The judge ordered for silence again. Everybody quieted down. At this time, the judge ordered the investigator to stand up. He talked about a bunch of nonsense stuff including the girl has lost her mind, she is very aggressive and arrogant, and she always wants to deny the truth. At this time, one of the audience members stood up, interrupted the investigator and asked. Are you a medical doctor and have you examined her? The judge ordered her to be seated. As soon as the lady said that, the crowd became noisy again. The judge who was getting kind of mad ordered the crowd to be silent again. Then the judge ordered the investigator to continue. The investigator repeated some stuff again and he added that the girl should be sent to a mental hospital. The judge ordered the investigator to sit down. Then the judge asked about a medical doctor. The medical doctor said that the convict is in a perfect health state. He also added the girl does everything deliberately and there is no sign of hallucination or anything. After the doctor finished, the same lady in the crowd stood up and she shouted to the people in the court room and said, now people did you just witness how fair our judgment system is. A very educated man who is supposed to be a very wise and smart man announced the convict as a mentally sick person. He is an investigator of the law and then a medical doctor said there is nothing wrong with the convict. Now use your judgment to evaluate our judgment system. The judge who was getting impatient ordered the crowd to be quiet.

After a delay, the judge asked about the convict's parents. Nobody knew about the parents even the convict. Finally, the judge announced "According to the law thieves, robbers, burglars, kidnappers, and hijackers are to be executed by burning in fire. Plus that, punishment for practicing witchcraft alone is death. That is why the court is not going to consider any reduction in punishment. Then they announced the exact date and time of the execution. As soon as the judge announced the decision about the convict, the same lady stood up in the middle of the crowd and shouted, this is not fair and she burst to cry "you all are a bunch of murderers", the lady continued. The convict was shocked, since she couldn't believe the outcome of the court case. Her eyes got full of tears, but neither the lady's complaint nor the convict's emotion was going to change the court's decision. People were ordered to leave the court room and the last person was the lady who still had eye contact with the girl. The convict didn't even know who she was and why she was so passionate about her.

The execution time arrived and the convict was brought to the execution place. A huge crowd had already gathered together in the place and some more were still coming. Someone was assigned to read a letter showing the convict's crimes. Also, the letter was talking about the court order for execution. The crowd was making so much noise. Another person was ordered to perform the execution. Some people in the crowd were passionate about the convict, but most of them were ruthless as if they had no heart. Some of the cruel people in the crowd were laughing as if nothing was about to happen. Some people in the crowd threw rotten tomatoes to the convict's face and then began to laugh and say yes, it's better now, you look much better now, they said. Some others began to laugh at this incident. It was a bizarre situation. Somebody in the crowd asked the convict if he could ask her a question. The convict was silent. The man didn't care about her response and said, there is a question in my mind that I haven't asked you for a long time. As soon as he said that he grabbed the crowd's attention and the people became silent. I was going to ask you if you are a witch or a bitch, the man asked sarcastically. The crowd burst to laughter. There was a lady in the crowd who was deeply sad and devastated, as if she was about to die. Her tears were dropping off her face while the rest of the crowd was maniacally excited. Somebody ordered the crowd to be quiet. The crowd was still noisy as if nobody was listening. At this time they were ordered to be quiet, louder than before. The crowd became quiet. The person who was responsible for reading the letter of conviction began to read. He was halfway through when a lady in the middle of the crowd interrupted him and she shouted, no, no wait, burn me in the fire instead, I'm ready to sacrifice myself. The people turned their head towards her and they looked at her strangely. After a little delay, the person who was reading the letter ordered the lady to be quiet. Please, please I beg you, the lady said instead of getting quiet. Didn't you hear what I just said? The reader asked very rudely. We are in the middle of processing the execution; do not interrupt us, the man continued. He began to read the rest of the letter. As soon as he finished, *somebody asked the convict if she had any words or final wishes to say. The convict who was shaking badly began to talk brokenly in a weak tone of voice. First I have a word with the lady who wanted to sacrifice herself, and second I want my doll facing me at the time of execution. Finally, I want something to write with. They brought the doll and a pen and gave them to the convict. She grabbed the doll and wrote something on the forehead, and then she put it on the ground a couple feet away. It took the lady in the crowd a while before she was able to pass through and reach the convict. The lady had a deep eye contact with the convict, as she was getting closer and closer, until she stopped. As the convict was looking at the lady's face very passionately she asked, m'aam may I ask why you were going to sacrifice yourself for me. I'm a mother, the lady said. I have a heart and I know what it's like to be a mother. I don't know where your mother is, but I'm sure if she was here she would have done the same thing, the lady continued. At this time one of the cruel guys said make it short, we don't have time forever. You look so familiar to me, the lady told the convict. Oh, do I? The convict asked. My mother was one of the best mothers in the world. She was so beautiful and kind, as if she was an angel. The convict continued. Then what happened? Where is she now? The lady asked. My destiny separated us, the convict said. Why? What happened? The lady asked. Don't ask me I can't tell, the convict replied. I know everybody has a private life and I don't want to be nosy, the lady said. Have you been thinking about her? The lady asked. Yes, of course, she was my life, she was my everything, the convict said. I can't even erase her from my memory and if you turn back you'll see my mom's name on the doll's forehead. I'll keep her in my heart and my memory until I die, the convict said pointing to the doll. The convict had not even finished yet when the lady fainted instantly right after looking at the doll's forehead. The name was Lisa. Two people grabbed Lisa by her shoulders and moved her away from the scene.*

Somebody brought some kerosene, and somebody in the crowd shouted yes it's good for her. I guess it's been a long time that she has not taken a bath, she really needs it and everybody began to laugh. The person in charge of execution closed the convict's eyes first, while she was crying. Then he poured a gallon of kerosene on the convict's head all the way to her toes. The fuel smelt nasty and the convict started to cough. Somebody in the crowd shouted it's good for you and us. We can celebrate around the fire in a minute, and everyone began to laugh. After they made sure the convict's body was wet, they set her on fire. Most people in the crowd began to clap. The blazes of fire burned the entire convict's body while she was screaming badly. She couldn't even move because they had already tied her up to a pole. The reflection of fire appeared in the doll's eyes and a thick black smoke spread all over the place.

"A Doll Which Belonged to a Witch". *It doesn't belong to a witch anymore, so go ahead and enjoy this precious antique.* This was the last page of the booklet, and Mary slammed the book shut after finishing it. Mary went into a deep thought, as if different feelings were challenging each other inside her head. First she got shocked due to the fact that she couldn't believe that somebody could have had such a miserable life. Then drops of tears appeared in the corner of her eyes. Indeed the story was really sad to her. She decided to return the doll, because a bad feeling told her that the doll must be cursed. She thought to herself that her son deserved a better gift than that. Then she thought that the doll may bring bad luck to her son, but all these thoughts went away from her head quickly and she changed her mind about returning the doll. Nonsense, she told herself. This is just one of those made up stories. It's really funny, who believes in witchcraft nowadays? She continued, thinking to herself. Only superstitious people may believe in those things, not the smart people, Mary thought to herself. She ended up putting the booklet away.

Mary rubbed her eyes a little bit since her eyes were getting a little tired of reading. Then she went to grab the paper of instructions. She wanted to pull the batteries out of its back. She read the instructions carefully. She took a quick look at the doll's eyes first, then she took the doll's clothes off (following the instructions). Then she found the battery place on the back of the doll, and she got a screw driver ready in hand to unscrew the lid. There were four screws. After opening the lid Mary pulled the batteries out of the place. There were two double A ones in there. Then as if she had done a hard and risky job; she took a deep breath. After all that, Mary went to her book shelf, and she ripped a sheet of paper off an unused journal. After that she got a pen ready and wrote something very neatly on the sheet of paper. Next, she folded the paper and she put it in the battery space carefully. Then she put the lid back on the battery place, and she screwed it back on the doll. She put the doll's clothes back on. After everything was done Mary packed up for her trip to visit her son.

In the meanwhile, Max and Sara were arranging to visit Grandma Martha, coincidentally. Anyways Mary arrived earlier than Max and the stepmom. Mary rang the bell and little John who was playing in the backyard rushed to the entry door. As soon as he opened the door he was thrilled to see his mom by the door. John jumped in between his mother's arms and they began to kiss each other. The three-year-old John's face got wet a little bit. That was Mary's tears on his face. It was like Mary didn't even want to stop kissing her son, but eventually she had to. She put him down, to grab the suitcases. As soon as she put John down, she saw

Grandma Martha standing by the door. They both hugged each other tightly. "I missed you all", Mary said. "We missed you too", Grandma Martha said. "How have you all been doing?" Mary said excitedly. "Don't worry we will tell you after you bring your stuff inside", grandma Martha said. Grandma Martha tried to help Mary, but she didn't let her and Mary brought her heavy suit cases in by herself. "You've grown up a lot since the last time I saw you", Mary told her son. "Yes he's like a big boy now", grandma Martha said. John was running around his mom due to extreme excitement. "He is so excited, can you tell?" Grandma Martha told Mary. "Yes, of course, I'm even more excited than him", Mary replied. "I haven't seen him for a long time and I was dying to see him", Mary continued. "How old are you now?" Mary asked her son. "3", the little John replied. "Oh my sweet heart, do you know how much I missed you?" Mary asked. John shook his head as a sign that he didn't know the answer to his mom's question. "As much as a whole world", Mary answered her own question. She hugged her son again. John quit walking around her mother all of a sudden and asked "what did you bring for me mom?" "I got a surprise for you", Mary said. "I love surprises", John said. "What is it mom?" John asked. "Take a guess", Mary replied. "It's a car toy", John said. "No you missed", Mary said. "You can take another guess", Mary continued. "I don't know",

John said. "Are you sure you don't want to take your second guess?" Mary asked. "Yes, I'm sure" John said, while everybody was looking at them. "Okay, if you are sure that you don't want to take a second guess; you are going to have to be patient. I've got to find it, it's somewhere in one of the suitcases", Mary continued. "John, don't you want to wait? Maybe she is tired now and she wants to sleep a little", grandpa said. "No it's okay I'm fine", Mary said. "I just have to find it, to be honest with you. I forgot in which one of the suitcases I put it in", Mary continued. "Don't worry Mom, I'll help you find it", John said. "Oh my sweet heart, you're so kind", Mary said. While Mary and John were digging in the suitcases, all of a sudden Mary found the doll box, which she had wrapped carefully. "Okay, now you should close your eyes", Mary told her son. "Why? John asked. As I told you, it's a surprise, that's why", Mary replied. "Okay I close my eyes and count to 10", John said. "Is that okay?" John asked. "Sure, 10 is enough", Mary responded. "1, 2, 3, John counted all the way to 10", while Mary was getting the doll out of the box and ready in her hands. "10", John counted the last number and he opened his eyes. As soon as he opened his eyes he saw a beautiful doll lying on his mother's hands. John got so excited and jumped to grab the doll out of her mother's hands. Mary moved her hands back a little bit and whispered, "Hush she is sleeping you don't want to wake her up, do you?" Mary said. John stopped moving instantly as he heard his mom. John put his finger in front of his nose in order to copy his mom and then he said hush likewise. "When did she sleep?" John asked. "I'm not sure, but anyways it's not a good idea to wake up anyone who is asleep", Mary answered. "How could I know when she's going to wake up?" John asked. "I don't know maybe sometime soon, but before then you'd better grab her and put it on your bed", Mary replied while everybody in the room was listening to their conversation, trying not to laugh. John took what his mother told him very seriously and listened to her. When he went to his room, everybody started to laugh. When John came back everybody was quiet. "Why were you laughing, what was funny?" John asked. Before they were able to answer the question they heard the bell. "I go, I go", John repeated. "Okay just be careful, don't run", Mary said. "He is a very smart boy", Martha said while John was heading towards the door. "I know, he's my son", Mary said. They were able to look through the window and see what was going on. They saw Max bringing John on the back of his shoulder. Sara was with him too. Everybody rushed to the door to greet and welcome them. Max was talking to John and he was laughing in the middle of talking too. Sara had a fake smile on her face, of course everybody could tell that. That was probably the best she could do, and the rest was out of her control. "How are you doing mother?" Sara asked Martha. She was used to referring to her mother in law as mother. Maybe she thought it was a perfect way to spoil her. Martha was smarter than what Sara thought. Martha knew Sara as someone who ruined her son's life, but she needed to take a lot of things into consideration. "I'm doing fine my sweet girl", Martha responded. "How about you?" Martha asked. "Well, it was a long trip, other than that everything was alright", Sara replied. Then it was Max's turn to greet and hug. "What's up mom? I missed you", Max said. "Me too son, why did you come back for a visit so late?" Martha asked. "You know how life is Mom, we were so busy", Max replied. "You should always have time for visiting your mother, shouldn't you?" Martha said. "I know what you're thinking, but I'll explain it to you later", Max said. Grandpa was not as sociable as Martha; that's why the greeting part for him didn't take too long. Then it came to Mary's turn. It was her very first time to see the poisonous snake having beautiful skin. "How do you do?" Sara introduced herself, stretching her arm to shake hands with Mary. Mary had a bad feeling, or better to say she had a bitter guess. She guessed the lady must be John's step mom; Mary guessed right but she was not sure yet. "How do you do?" Mary said, shaking hands with Sara. As soon as Max saw his ex-wife he got embarrassed a little bit, but he did his best to control himself and he tried to overcome his feelings and emotions. At the time for a few seconds Max lost his power of judgment, and he couldn't decide what to do. What shall I do now? Max kept asking himself. What if Sara figures out about my ex-wife? Hiding the truth can sometimes be troublesome. "Mom, I think the doll should be awake by now don't you think so", John asked Mary. While doing this, he interrupted his dad's thoughts. Everybody looked at John at this time. "I'm not sure, we can check in a minute", Mary answered. As soon as Sara heard that, her face changed. There was a slight smile on her face before but not anymore. A gigantic power of jealousy was trying to kill her and Sara was trying to struggle and survive. Sara's face turned red due to extreme anger, but at the same time she was trying not to be a victim of jealousy. It was really hard for her to win the battle, but finally she did. "Are you doing alright girl?" grandpa who was a very smart man said. At the time everyone was watching John but the grandpa. Grandpa was a good inspector. He liked navigating everywhere to make sure everything was alright. "Yes, yes I'm doing fine", Sara said as if grandpa shocked her a bit. "I don't think so, you look sick", grandpa said. At this moment everyone's attention got diverted towards Sara. "It's okay. I'm fine", Sara said. "Let's get inside and I'll rinse my face a little bit". John was gone by then, and everyone else helped move the luggage inside. "What happened Sara, are you okay?" Max asked. "How many times should I tell you? I'm fine, leave me alone", Sara whispered. "I'm sorry, I was just trying to help", Max said. They whispered so quietly that nobody heard them. "So, she is the princess", Sara whispered sarcastically. "I've told you before, there's nothing in between us anymore", Max said and put his suitcases inside on the floor.

Sara went to the restroom. She felt so sick that she began to throw up. When she finished she looked so pale, by the time she came back everybody was busy with something. Grandpa was watching TV. Max was drinking water, and Martha was whispering something into Mary's ears. When Sara came back she looked like a stranger. Sara found a seat in the corner of the room and rested in there. Max who drove all the way was feeling a little tired; he took a quick look at Sara's face and asked her if she wanted to drink something. Sara didn't show any reaction at all; she was sick and mad. Grandma Martha and Mary were still whispering something. Mary tried to take a quick look at Sara's face without getting her attention. It was like Sara was looking at the middle of nowhere. "Do you want to go and get some rest?" Grandma Martha came out and said. "No thank you, I'm fine." by the time Sara said that; John rushed out of a room having the doll in his hands. He went straight to his mom, without even paying a slight attention to his stepmom. "Mom look, I brought her with me. I guess she is awake now", John said. "Oh my sweetie, are you sure she is awake?" Mary asked. "Yes she opened her eyes when I moved her a little bit", John said. "Oh really?" Mary asked. "Yes she did", John said. "Okay now you can go and play with her", Mary said. "Yes mom, that's what I'm going to do", John said. After that he went straight to Sara. "My mother bought me this", John said and showed it to Sara. Sara who got extremely jealous said "Wow look at that it's so beautiful. Can I take a look at it?" Sara said. "Sure, here you are", John said very politely. He gave the doll to Sara. Sara kept looking at the doll for a little bit and said. "I love this doll so much, it's gorgeous, can it be mine?" Sara asked. "No, my mom bought the doll for me. You can ask your mom to buy you one", John replied. "I know, but yours looks so much prettier", Sara said. "I know but I cannot give it to you, my mom bought it for me only. Isn't that right mom?" John asked Mary. Mary said, "Tell her you can keep it for a while and then give it back to me." John listened to his mom and copied her word for word. "You know what though; tell her I thought dolls were for girls, not boys." Sara told John. John repeated what he was told. "I was in a hurry, and I couldn't find anything better than that", Mary said embarrassed. "We can do something", Sara said. "Like what?" John asked. "I've got some car toys and we can exchange them", Sara said. "What does exchange mean?" John asked. "It means the car toys would be yours and the doll would be mine", Sara replied. "No I don't want it", John said. "How about a bicycle?" Max said interrupting. "Hmm, let me think, is it a good one?" John asked. "Yes it's awesome", Max replied. At this time John turned back and asked about his mother's opinion. "I don't know sweetie, it's your decision", Mary responded. "You have plenty of time to think about it, don't worry", Max said and John got the doll back from Sara. Sara who was not able to tolerate the situation any longer asked her husband if they could leave as soon as possible. "What's the matter with you? We drove a long way here for visiting my parents. Now you want me to leave as soon as possible?" Max asked angrily. "Okay, okay didn't you hear me? I said as soon as possible, I didn't say now." Sara said. "Don't you like my parents?" Max asked. "Well that's not the reason", Sara replied. "So what is the reason?" Max asked. "Oh now I know, my ex-wife is bothering you", without even waiting for Sara's response. "Are you going to keep your promise?" Max asked. "Promise about what?" Sara asked. "Come on now, don't you remember? This time John is going to live with us, are you ready?" Sara who was trying to pretend and act as a passionate mother said, "Of course;

I'm going to take care of John as if he is my own son." As a matter of fact Sara had a really hard time to make such a quick answer. She was feeling mad on the inside and showing happy on the outside. "Good, so we leave as soon as possible", Max said.

Mary decided to leave; she was feeling the same as Sara and she thought that she had no reason to stay any longer. One day she came to John and told him that she was about to leave. John burst to cry. He was saying something, but he was crying so loud that even his mother had a hard time to understand what he was saying. "Okay, okay stop it, you are going to be a man soon. You shouldn't cry", Mary said. "I don't want you to leave; I want you to stay with me", John said. "I'm going to come and see you again, don't worry honey", Mary said while embracing her son. "Why don't you come with us?" John asked. "I wish I could but I can't", Mary replied. "Why?" "Because my husband is alone by himself and he is waiting for me", Mary responded. "You can come together with us", John said."Just listen to your mom and be a good boy, Okay?" Mary said and she kissed her son with eyes full of tears. "Why are you crying mom?" John asked. "No, I'm okay", Mary said and she kissed her son again. "What do you want me to do with the doll?" John asked. "As I told you it's yours; I'm happy with whatever you'd like to do with it", Mary said. "Now let me go, I'm late", Mary continued and she said bye to everyone and left. John was still crying and everyone was trying to calm him down.

Max who was trying to get the sad thoughts out of John's head said, "The bicycle is coming soon, are you ready?" "Where is it now?" John who was still crying said brokenly. "It is on its way. Soon it's going to be yours, aren't you happy?" Max asked. John, who was not crying as bad as before, shook his head up and down as a sign of yes. "Good, so the doll is going to be ours right?" Max asked. At this time John didn't say anything for seconds and then he said I'm not sure yet. "It's okay, you can still have the bicycle while you are trying to decide", Max said very kindly and kissed his son.

While Mary was there Max was feeling ashamed of himself, so ashamed that he didn't even talk to her. He was trying to avoid even a simple eye contact as if he didn't know Mary. When she left Max and Sara felt much more comfortable than before.

In about a few days after Mary left, Max and his wife decided to leave too. When they came John was not with them, but when they were going back home they planned on taking him. It was mostly what Max had planned. Sara hated John, and she just pretended to love John for Max. If she didn't, then she would have messed up her family relationship. In that situation Mary acted like a very strong magnet opposed to the other magnet which was Max. Mary's magnet was so strong that John got completely attracted to it, since she was the real mother. Mary's magnet was so strong that John wanted his mom to be with him. Then it was like Mary took the magnet away from him and just because of legal matters and some financial and family problems, she had to throw the magnet away. She had to do this using her own hands and since she didn't want to suffer anymore due to the decision she made, she decided to leave. Therefore, this doesn't show any proof that the promises Max made such as buying a bicycle and so and so was a stronger magnet than the mother's magnet.

One day, Max went to his son and asked him if he was ready to go with them. In other words, he took advantage of a three-year-old by judgment, and said if your answer is yes, the bicycle would be coming soon. Otherwise they would leave him with Grandma Martha, and he added that there would be an unclear future for John if he would stay with grandma. In other words, Max was somehow trying to scare his three-year-old son about his future. Anyways his trick worked and after a unilateral conversation, John simply said yes. A smile appeared on the father's face and Max decided to tell Sara about John right away.

Sara and Max went back to John and they told him you are a smart boy and they told him that they are leaving soon. They told Grandma Martha about their decision and they left the day after. Grandma Martha was so worried about her only grandson, and she was not sure about what would happen to John in the future. She was always thinking that John could have a dark future, living with his stepmom. Grandma Martha was kind of old and she knew a lot of things about Sara and what she had done by then. Plus that, Grandma Martha was a type of person having a strong feeling of sixth sense. Anyways before they were about to leave grandma Martha gave some advice about John to her son. "Promise me that you are going to take good care of him", Grandma Martha said. "I promise and don't worry about him", Max said. "God is not going to forgive you if you forget and ignore your son just because of your selfishness or anything else", Grandma Martha said. "I know that Mom, I'm not a baby anymore. I don't need such advices", Max said. "Yes, I do know that you are my smart boy, but I also know that even the smartest people can sometimes be deceived", Grandma Martha said. "Okay, okay, I just told you mom, don't worry", Max said. "I was going to just remind you and remember being a good father is not easy, but once you are a good father your place would be in heaven", Grandma Martha said and she kissed her son on his face. Max did the same thing in return. As a last word grandma Martha said, "Always try to compensate for the mistakes you've made in the past. May God forgive you", Grandma Martha said. "Yes mom", Max said, and then Grandma Martha gave some pieces of advice to Sara about John. Including taking care of him as if he is her real son and not looking at him as a step son. "I promise", Sara said. Then it was John's turn, "When are you coming back to see me?" Grandma Martha asked John. At this time, John took a quick look at his dad's face in order to get some help. "Tell her sometime soon", Max helped his son. John copied his dad word for word and everybody laughed. "You promise your granny to be a good boy", John nodded. "We are going to buy him a bicycle, did you know that?" "Wow, no I did not", Grandma Martha replied. "You can ride your bicycle here to see us right?" Grandma asked. John nodded again with a sweet smile on his face and everybody laughed again. At this time, Max faced his dad and said, "Dad take care of yourself and sorry for all the bother." "There was no bother at all son; actually we enjoyed being together for a while", grandpa said. "Are you going to come for a visit?" Max asked his dad. "We are coming but I'm not sure when yet", grandpa replied. Max's dad was older than his mother and his health condition was not as good as Grandma Martha. Maybe that's why he said he was not sure. Anyways they said goodbye to each other, and the page of John's life turned into an unexpected tragedy.

The next day after their arrival began with revisiting their family doctor. Sara was unable to have her own child. Their doctor had already told them about that, but they didn't want to give up. That's why they wanted to make sure if a miracle had happened for Sara, which was her pregnancy. Unfortunately though, this time the result was negative too. "Doctor, please do something for me", Sara said. "Money is not our problem, we can pay you as much as it takes", Sara continued. "I'm sorry to tell you there is no way", the doctor said. "Since you want to have your own baby as you told me before", the doctor continued. "Of course I want my own baby. There is no doubt about it", Sara said. "Does it really matter honey?" Max asked his wife. "Of course it does, somebody else's baby is never going to be like your own baby", Sara responded. "So you mean John is not important to you, right?" Max asked. "Well, I didn't say that, you know what I'm talking about", Sara replied. "Not exactly, but I'm trying to understand what you mean", Max said. "Do you think there is much of a difference?" Max asked. "As a matter of fact, yes I do", Sara replied. "Did you know that so many families who are unable to have their own children adopt kids?" Max asked. "Yes, but I'm not one of them", Sara replied. "So you think that you are more important and better than them, right?" Max asked. "No, I didn't mean that", Sara said as she was trying to hide the truth. "Besides that,

I'm not in an argument mood now", Sara continued. "I'm not arguing with you", Max said. "I was just trying to talk about facts", Max continued. "So you mean that I'm lying right? What kind of fact is that", Sara asked. At this time Max remained silent. Maybe he didn't want to say anything, or maybe he didn't have anything to say. "Well, let's change the subject", Max said. "We always have the same argument over and over", Max continued. At this time Sara burst to tears as if she was controlling herself for a long time. "Please do something", Sara told her husband while she was still crying. "We are trying honey, you know that", Max said. "I promise you, we are not going to give up, at the same time we should pray too", Max continued. "I have prayed a lot, but no results so far", Sara said. "Maybe it's not in God's will", Max said. "Now let's go home, John is alone. You can look at him as a gift from God. Maybe there is something to this problem that we are not aware of. Or maybe this thing is going to benefit us, somehow or someway", Max continued. "You are a master at changing the subject, you know that, right?" Sara asked and they both laughed and they went back home.

By the time they arrived, little John was playing with his doll. As soon as John saw his dad and step mom coming in, he jumped excitedly and ran towards his dad. As if his dad was the only person there, and he paid no attention to his step mom. "Did you buy me the bicycle dad? You remember, you promised", John said. "Of course he promised you, but you remember if you give the doll to us, we can give the bicycle to you." The stepmom replied without giving even a little time for Max to answer the question. "Take it easy honey", Max interrupted. "He is just a little boy, don't take it too hard on him", Max continued. "I'm not taking it hard, but a promise is a promise", Sara said. "Yes that's right, but we also told him he can keep the doll for a while to make up his mind", Max said. "Yes but tell him that not too long, we can't wait that long", Sara said. "Are you becoming a baby?" Max asked his wife. "No, why?" Sara asked. "Because you're acting like a baby", Max replied. "You know I am kind of offended", Sara said. "Wow I didn't know being a baby is offensive", Max said. "If this is the case, why are you so interested in having your own baby?" Max continued. "What does that have to do with anything?" Sara asked. "I told you that you are a master at changing the subject", Sara continued without even letting her husband talk. "Okay, okay, that's enough we can't keep fighting in front of a kid", Max whispered. "Well my boy, I know that I promised you, but I haven't got the chance to buy the bicycle for you. I do promise that I'll get it soon." Max told his son. "When?" John asked. At this time Sara who was getting really jealous interfered and said as soon as you keep your promise. John looked at Sara's face hatefully, since he figured out what kind of person he's going to be dealing with for a long time. "Don't worry son, you can keep your doll as long as you want", Max said with a smile on his face. Sara was not happy at all. That's why she was about to say something, but Max didn't let her and he pulled her arm and said take it easy. Sara took a look at her husband's face and she decided not to say anything.

When Sara and Max went away John grabbed his doll and he took a meaningful look at the doll's face. The doll helped John refresh his memory about his mother. John really wanted his mother to be with him. Every time he looked at the doll, it reminded him of his mother. The more he looked at the doll, the clearer his mother's picture became. John was really sad, and nobody knew how sad he was but him.

So many problems were surrounding Max and his family. Problems such as recession in the economy and business. Sara was not able to have her own baby. John as a step son in the family, which resulted in an atmosphere of jealousy. The doll which was spreading the atmosphere of animosity in the family. As a matter of fact Sara who did not want to see the doll as a sign of John's real mom, tried to provoke Max against his son. On the other hand, Sara wanted to use the doll as a cover on her disability of having her own child. Sara used the doll as a tool to picture her imaginary baby in her mind. Of course Sara didn't want to see any signs of Mary in her family, and if they had to keep the doll Sara wanted to keep it and imagine the things the way she wanted. Even if she had to tamper with the facts. The job of course was not an easy one for Sara and it required a very well calculated plan. An atmosphere of distrust between Max and Sara was an additional problem. This also added to the mentioned problems.

Due to the nature of business that Max had; he had to travel a lot and he couldn't take his family with him on his trips. Sara took advantage of this situation and she left John home alone frequently.

One day Sara left John home alone early in the morning and she went for shopping. When Sara left home; John was sleeping. It was 8 a.m., and all of a sudden John woke up because of a nightmare he had. He dreamt that he had lost his doll. As soon as he woke up he rushed to the place that he normally put his doll. The problem was that it wasn't there. His heart began to beat fast. John searched everywhere in his room, but the doll was nowhere to be found. The more he looked for the doll, the faster his heartbeat was. This was giving him so much stress. He was mad and sad. He was getting impatient and agitated. He wanted to pull his hair and break everything into pieces. John got frustrated and disappointed since his efforts were futile.

Then he burst to cry as if he had controlled himself for years. His nightmare became a reality. While he was crying the idea of calling to his step mom came to his mind. "Sara! Sara! Sara!" John shouted louder and louder. There was no one home to answer him back. This increased the level of his stress and madness. He was really upset now. At this time John decided to look around in the rooms to find Sara. At the same time he called out to his step mom, but it was useless. The more he looked, the less he found. Now another thing added to his problems. First he couldn't find his doll and now he couldn't find his step mom. Now he was getting more and more scared as time went by. John got so scared that he had stopped crying and shouting by then. It is really a bad mistake to leave a kid home alone. The first thing John did was getting inside his room and locking the door. He jumped on his bed, leaning against the wall John took a quick look around then he day dreamed about his beloved doll. It is unusual for boys to like dolls, but John's situation was an exception. The doll was a gift from his mother and since John was away from his mother the doll was working as a symbol of love. Anytime John looked at his doll, he could picture his mother's face, but now there was no doll to bring his mother's picture to him. This meant that John had to do the entire job by himself. No wonder he had a hard time to do it. The four-year-old John laid on his bed and thought about his past for a long time until he fell asleep again with an empty stomach.

The clock on the wall struck 9:00 p.m. Sara was not back yet. As soon as John heard the clock, he woke up. It took him a while before he remembered what had happened to him that day. A flash of memories sparkled in his mind. The flash brought the picture of his doll back to him again. At this time John rubbed his eyes and he took a look around. He sharpened his ears to hear things better. It was the end of summer, that's why the days were shorter than before. John went to the window and pulled his blinds enough to be able to see outside. It was absolutely dark out there. No noise could be heard except for the clock noise. As soon as John noticed the darkness out there he got scared more than before. He thought to himself that maybe his stepmom was back by then. That's why he decided to call out to her again. "Sara! Sara! Sara!" each time louder than before. He didn't hear anything back. John was too scared to get out of his room, but after a long challenge between him and his feelings, he overcame and he decided to go out. He unlocked the door very slowly and then he opened the door. The door made a little squeaky noise, but it didn't matter because John was not paying attention to it. Anyways John stepped out of the room and he wanted to call to Sara, but at first he hesitated to do that. Perhaps he was still too scared. Maybe a stranger or intruder could hear him and they would come after him, but anyways John prevailed again and he called out to Sara for several times. After each call he paused a little bit waiting for a response, but unfortunately he heard nothing. Sara was still out. The weather was getting kind of windy. That's why after the last call John heard a noise. He didn't realize the noise was coming from the tree branches outside scratching against the window. That's why anytime that the weather was windy, the trees made so much noise, but John didn't know that. The noise scared John to death. He thought there was a thief or somebody out there. At this time John was shaking and he didn't know what to do. It was like he couldn't shout either.

At this time the entry door opened all of a sudden and John screamed really badly. It ended up being Sara. Sara, who got shocked a little bit, came in and shut the door behind her. "What's wrong?" Sara asked in shock. John who had stopped screaming by then threw himself into Sara's arms as if he found the safest refuge in the world and then he burst to cry. For half a second Sara imagined that she was hugging her own child, but the feeling was temporary and volatile. All of a sudden Sara pushed John back and she frowned at him. "What's the matter with you crazy boy?" Sara said. John, who didn't expect such a bad welcome, got shocked. He couldn't believe what his eyes were witnessing and what his ears were hearing. "Okay now can you tell me what happened? I can't wait to hear", Sara said. John who was so scared didn't say a word. "Now you are driving me crazy, I asked you what the problem is", Sara said. This time though she didn't hear any reply from John, who was still staring at her. "Don't stare at me like that stupid boy", Sara said unashamed of herself because no one else could hear her. Max could be one of the best defenders, but unfortunately he was far away from home. John was still staring at Sara as if he couldn't understand a single word coming out of her mouth. "You don't want to answer my question right, wait till your dad comes back", Sara said. "I'm going to complain about your behavior", Sara continued. John who was extremely mad and he was still crying, ran to his room and slammed the door behind him. "Wait a minute, where are you going?" Sara called out to John. It was too late because John was too fast for Sara to catch. Sara went by John's room and she knocked on the door several times. These efforts were useless. John had locked the door and he wouldn't open it. "Open the door, I want to talk to you", Sara repeated a few times. John didn't answer. "I told you open the door, otherwise I'm going to tell your dad about you", Sara said. "If you don't open the door a big punishment is waiting for you", Sara continued. All the efforts were useless since John didn't listen to his stepmom. Sara got disappointed and she left him alone.

The next day Max came back home. It was around 11 a.m. As soon as he opened the door and stepped in; Sara heard him and she rushed to welcome him in. They hugged each other and the kisses came right after. "How are you darling?" Max asked. "I missed you a lot", Max continued. "I'm doing fine", Sara said. I "missed you too", Sara continued. "How is everything?" Max asked. "Everything is good", Sara replied. "How was the business?" Sara asked. "It was good but not as good as it used to be though", Max replied. "How come?" Sara asked. "You know, it's slow now and the economy is down", Max replied. Max was in the pharmaceutical business. Although in the recession time, sick people would still use medicines, but they try to use the least expensive ones. With that in mind, Max's business was not an exception. "Where is John by the way?" Max asked. "He is in his room", Sara replied. "Maybe he is playing with his toys", Sara continued. "Let me go and see what he is doing", Max said. At this time Sara held her husband's arm and stopped him from going. "Don't worry while you're changing your clothes, I'll go and bring him", Sara said. Sara asked in a casual way that didn't seem suspicious at all. "Okay go and tell him that your dad missed you a lot", Max said. "Okay, sit in your chair, I'm going to bring him to you", Sara said. John's room was a little far from the entry door, that's why they didn't call to each other from that distance. Sara who was getting nervous and not even sure what to do. She didn't know how she could bring John to his dad, or better to say how she could force him out of his room. She walked to the room, taking her time. She walked so slowly that she was able to find answers to her questions. She knew Max loved his son; that's why she had to act like a professional actor and she had to make up a believable story for her husband to provoke him against his son.

Everybody knows that women are really smart and there is no doubt about it. While Sara was deeply involved in her thoughts she found herself by John's room. Sara paused a little bit, as if she didn't even notice that she was there by the room already. Maybe she noticed it a little too late since she didn't have presence of mind. Anyways as soon as she was completely conscious of what she was doing, she knocked on the door. "John", Sara said in a low tone of voice. There was no answer. "John, open the door", Sara said raising her voice a little. This time there was no answer either. "John open the door, your dad is here", Sara said with a higher tone of voice impatiently. Sara waited for a response for about 5 seconds and she was almost about to call John for the fourth time. She didn't this time, since John interrupted her and he opened the door very slowly.

The door made a long squeaky noise. John was standing by the door, staring into Sara's eyes with a slight frown on his face. John looked like an innocent boy. About time, Sara said, as she was not happy at all. "I'm glad that you decided to open the door", Sara continued. "Quit staring at me like that", Sara said. "At least have a smile on your face. Aren't you happy? Your dad is here", Sara continued and she grabbed John's hand and dragged him slowly towards the room dad was sitting in. As soon as John saw his dad sitting in a chair from behind, he pulled his hand and he left his step mom behind. John who was really excited ran towards his dad with wide open arms, in order to hug him. By the time Max noticed the presence of his son, he opened his arms to embrace him. John was happy and sad at the same time. Happy because he saw his dad again and sad because of the events that happened to him after Max left. The kisses were coming fast as if they were racing. "How is my son doing?" Max asked while he was still kissing his son. "Don't make him too spoiled", Sara jealously said. "I haven't seen him in a long time, let me enjoy my time with him", Max said. "So tell me about your doll", Max said. "Did you play with it a lot?" Max asked his son while he had already stopped kissing him and he was looking into his son's eyes. As soon as Max reminded John of his doll; drops of tears appeared in the corners of John's eyes. Max sharpened his focus and he noticed the tears. "What happened?" Max asked. "Did I say something wrong?" Max asked. John, who was staring at his dad, didn't say anything. At this time Max turned around to ask his wife about John. "What's wrong with him?" Max asked. "Did anything happen while I was away?" Max continued impatiently waiting for an answer. Sara, who was not prepared well to answer the question, said "What happened, I don't know". "He is crying", Max told his wife. "Oh really, why"? Sara said as if she didn't know anything about what had happened before. "What's the matter John?" Sara asked John, trying to prove that she didn't know anything about the situation. John still had eye contact with his dad's eyes and he didn't even bother himself to look at Sara. John was still silent. "Come on, tell me if anything is bothering you", Max said. "Remember a man never cries", Max continued. At this time John, who was feeling the burden of the whole world on him, made a strange noise. A noise which was in no way understandable. A noise which sounded like the way dumb people talk. "Are you okay son?" Max asked. After a little pause, John made the same weird noise, but this time it was longer than before. Max who was trying hard to understand something out of what John was trying to say, got frustrated, since all his efforts were useless. "Do you understand what he is saying?" Max asked Sara who was watching them carefully. "No, not really", Sara responded. "Tell me the truth, what's going on?" Max asked with curiosity. "I swear, I don't know", Sara replied. "He is just a crazy boy, I don't know what has happened to him", Sara continued. "But he was okay when I left", Max said. "Yes I know, that's how kids are", Sara said. "One day they are okay and the next day they are not", Sara continued. "I hope it's not a serious problem", Max said. "Don't you worry, I told you kids are like that", Sara said. "Trust me, women know kids more than men", Sara continued. "I hope so", Max said. "I know so", Sara said. "Just wait, soon he is going to talk more than both of us", Sara said with a slight smile on her face as she was trying to convince her husband. "Well, let's see", Max said. "Yes you will see and don't spoil him too much", Sara said in an imperative tone of voice. When Max heard that he didn't say anything else and he left John and Sara alone.

Max decided to sit in a chair and watch the news. Sara went to the kitchen to prepare dinner and John who was very sad went back to his room. Dinner was ready in about an hour. Sara called to everyone to be ready for dinner. If one looked in Sara's face, they could tell that she was thinking deeply. Everyone got in the kitchen but John. Maybe he didn't hear Sara. This time Max decided to go and bring him. "Let me go and bring him", Max said. "Okay", Sara said. Max went by John's room and he knocked on the door for a few times. He waited for a few seconds for a response, but he didn't hear anything. Max tried to turn the door knob, but he couldn't since it was locked. This time Max called to John. "John open the door, it's me", Max said. In about a second and a half, the door opened. John was standing by the opened door. John was looking into his father's eyes and Max did the same thing for about 5 seconds. "Aren't you hungry?" Max asked. John nodded innocently. "Good, let's go then, dinner is ready", Max said and he grabbed his son's hand. On their way to the kitchen Max asked John, "You still don't want to talk to me?" After a short pause, John made the same strange noise that he had made before. "What?" Max asked. "What did you just say?" Max continued. Asking questions were of no use since John's answers were nothing but making noises like animals. Now they were in the kitchen sitting by the table. Max asked Sara, "You still don't want to tell me what happened."

Praying caused a lot of unexpected trouble for Sara since she could no longer convince her husband of John's situation. Since they both heard the mumbling in the praying time. This proved to the parents that John had a problem, but neither of them was sure about the nature of the problem. At this time Sara who was losing her control and confidence began to talk about what had happened brokenly. The more Sara talked, the angrier her husband became. John was watching both of them. When Sara finished, Max lost his control and he burst out yelling at Sara. "You left him home alone for one whole day?" Max asked. "How could you do that to a little kid?" Max continued. "I'm sorry, I'm sorry", Sara said. "You're sorry? I'm sorry too, sometimes being sorry is useless." Max said sarcastically. "I promise, it won't happen again", Sara said. "You know if it happens again you're not going to see us anymore", Max said. Sara who was feeling like a loser in the battle said, "I promise. Even this time I didn't do it on purpose. My shopping took a long time", Sara said while she was shaking. "How long does it take to shop? One hour, two hours, three hours, not the whole day, that's ridiculous", Max said. "Yes you're right", Sara said. John who was still watching his parents was shaking. When Max noticed that he tried to control himself and he lowered his voice. "It's okay we're just discussing some issues", Max told John. "You can finish your food and go to bed", Max continued. Everybody became silent at this time, and they started having dinner. John ate a little bit and then he kissed his dad only and he went to bed. "Don't forget to brush your teeth", Max told his son.

"We should take him to a speech therapist", Max said. "Maybe it's a serious problem", Max continued. Sara who was guilty but didn't like to accept it remained silent. "Don't you have a tongue in your mouth?" Max asked. "Maybe you became mute too", Max continued.

"Yes", Sara said. "Yes what? Are you mute?" Max asked. "No I meant we should take him to a doctor", Sara replied. "Good, now tell me how he got scared when you came back home", Max said. "I don't know; I just heard an ear piercing scream when I opened the door", Sara responded. "Hmm of course he gets scared, because he is just a little kid." It was like Max answered his own question. "We should book an appointment with a speech therapist tomorrow." Max said. "Okay", Sara said, and they both went to bed. The next day they booked an appointment for a speech therapist. To make it short even the speech therapist couldn't do anything and this situation made Max angrier than before, and Sara was being pushed to the corner. Sara had to think of a way to bring the situation back to normal. That was not an easy job at all. The only way that Sara could think of doing that was giving the doll back to John, but she had to prepare herself for doing that.

One day Sara called to John and told him that she found the doll under her king size bed and she gave it to John. As soon as John saw his doll he got very excited and a big smile appeared on his face, a smile that hadn't come on his face for a long time. Sara was pretending to be happy too. The strange noises came again, but this time the noise was due to happiness and excitement. "What?" Sara asked. John made the same strange noise again. It was not possible to understand even a single word of what John was trying to say. "What did you just say?" Sara asked. "Ok that's enough. You just need to be thankful that I found your doll." As soon as Sara said that, John became silent, staring into Sara's face. "Aren't you happy, don't tell me that you are not", Sara said. "I have some more good news for you too. Don't you want to hear?" Sara asked. John remained silent while holding the doll very tightly. "Well I'm going to make your doll a nice dress, how is that?" Sara asked. A sweet smile appeared on John's face. "Now I'm sure you are happy? Aren't you." Sara asked. Sara was trying to make John talk by any means. "I'm going to find some fabrics and I'm going to start it soon", Sara said. Max and Sara did anything they could so John would be able to talk again, like before. The days passed by and John was growing more and more.

One day that Sara was not in a good mood at all, decided to pick on John again. That day she was thinking about her life and why she couldn't have her own kid. That was not an unusual thing because the thoughts came to her mind once in a while, but her frustration that day was worse than usual. Sara called to John and picked on him about his room. "Look at you. Look at your room; how many times do I have to tell you that your room should be clean and organized?" Sara said. "Your room is nasty, and I think the only thing you care about is your doll. Yeah that's right, just your doll", Sara repeated. John was so scared of Sara's tone of voice and he was staring into Sara's eyes. "You are not a baby anymore. You are five years old, and you should know much better than that", Sara continued. "You know what; I'm getting sick of this situation. Now I'm going to give you a good lesson. I'm going to take your doll away from you until you learn that you should be organized." As soon as John heard that he mumbled something and some wrinkles appeared on his face. It was like a combination of frowning and crying. "Now what?" Sara asked. "If you think you can get your doll back with that face, you're wrong", Sara said. "The only way is to arrange your room neatly", Sara continued. At this time drops of tears appeared in the corners of John's eyes. "Look at you." Sara said sarcastically. "No wonder your Mom gave you a doll as a gift. Now I know why, because you're not even a boy because boys don't cry", Sara said. "Yes boys don't play with dolls", Sara continued. "You should be ashamed of yourself. Now I'm going to hide this somewhere until you behave." Sara said and went away.

At this time John decided to chase after his step mom. Yes he really wanted to know where she was taking the doll, but he had to be extremely careful. The slightest mistake could turn the whole situation into a disaster.

Max was away again for business purposes, and this was a perfect opportunity for Sara to do whatever she wanted to, without fear of her husband. John waited until Sara was far enough so that she wouldn't be able to see him.

It was 8:00 p.m. John took very careful steps when following Sara. Sara went to her bedroom and closed the door and John went back to his room. John was quite satisfied, since now he knew where to look for his doll. John waited for the right time so that he could get his doll back. Patience is a very good thing. That night Sara didn't come back from her bed room and John didn't either.

That night was one of the scariest nights John had in his entire life. That was because of a terrible nightmare he had. He dreamt of his stepmom making fun of him in front of his friends. She was laughing at him like an evil movie character. She kept saying what boy in the world plays with a doll. The nightmare was too scary for John's age. That's why he couldn't see the whole thing and he woke up.

It was 2:00 after midnight and John's heart was beating fast. He got up and sat in his bed for a short time. The night light in his room helped him not to get scared very much. All of a sudden something came to his mind while his body was still shaking a little bit. The thought was about the doll. Was he deciding to do something? He opened the door very quietly so it wouldn't make much noise. He stepped forward, heading towards Sara's bedroom. There was a combination of fear and madness in John's spirit. He was just five years old and of course that was too much for a kid of that age.

Step by step he got closer and closer until John found himself by his stepmom's bedroom. John lifted his right arm very slowly and carefully until he touched the knob. Everywhere was quiet, and of course that's not an unusual thing at midnight. John turned the knob, but the knob didn't move. It seemed like the door was locked. As soon as John noticed that he got really frustrated and disappointed. What else could he do besides being patient? He came back to his bedroom and for some reason he learned something indirectly. He locked the door. He was sick of other people touching his private belongings.

The next day on accident John found his stepmom's room door open. His stepmom was cooking in the kitchen. That was a perfect opportunity for him to search for his doll. He needed to be really careful though. The good thing was that Sara normally spent alone time for cooking. In other words, she was very meticulous about it, but still John had to be very careful regardless, since the only telephone they had was in the bedroom. So he should pray for no phone calls. The first thing John did was locking his own room so that his step mom would think he was still in his room and that's what he did. With quiet steps he got closer and closer to the bedroom. John was not able to justify his stepmom's behavior in any way. That's why he had the courage to do such a thing. On his way he was thinking why his stepmom makes fun of him so much.

Anyways, John entered the bedroom without even having to open the door, since it was already open. The first thing he did was pulling the telephone cord from the outlet. Yes he was smart enough to do that. Then he started searching and digging in everywhere. Including the cabinet, drawers, and under the bed, until he found the doll under the huge bed. He really had a hard time finding the doll because the space under the bed was badly cramped and he had to crawl in between the stuff. He did it anyway and as soon as he did, he rushed back to his room. He got really lucky since nothing wrong happened, except for one thing that we will get to.

The next day Max came back from his trip and he opened the door. His face was not as happy as before and one could tell that easily. "What was the problem?" Sara and John both had no idea, until the conversation started. After normal hugs and kisses; he questioned Sara for not answering the phone calls. Sara had no idea what he was talking about. "What phone calls? I didn't hear any phone calls at all", Sara said. Not once, not twice, but about ten times, Max said. Sara was really surprised. "Did you even leave a message?" Sara asked. "I couldn't", Max replied. "I thought you were talking on the phone so long that I didn't even get a chance to talk", Max continued. "Are you kidding me?" Sara asked. "No, no kidding, as a matter of fact I'm very serious", Max said. "Next time would you please cut the crap and let other people call too", Max continued. "I swear I don't know. What are you talking about?" Sara asked. "I definitely know what I'm talking about", Max said. "Maybe there is an emergency. Maybe somebody is dying. Not one hour, not two hours, not 3, but anytime I called I wasn't able to get ahold of you. Isn't that funny?" Max said while he was raising his voice. "Okay you just came home and you're tired, now just take a deep breath and relax. This is not good for your health at all", Sara said. Max listened spontaneously. "No, serious, you tell me if I'm wrong", Max continued. "I hear you, but don't worry we're going to figure it out", Sara said. "Now tell me what you were going to tell me over the phone", Sara continued. "I was going to tell you that I was going to come back later than I was supposed to, and I didn't want you to worry about me. Instead I got worried about you", Max said. "Now I'm happy that you came back safe", Sara said in a tone of voice indicating that she got bored of that conversation.

To make it short when Sara went to the bedroom she checked the phone out of curiosity. Her husband was right, the phone was unplugged. As soon as she noticed that she went into a deep thought, trying to figure out how that happened. Her sixth sense told her to check under the bed. Yes, she was looking for the doll, but she had no luck in finding it. Right after that she hurried to John's room, but she found the door locked and she started calling to John. "John? John!" she repeated. "Open the door", Sara continued. Since John didn't like Sara he didn't even bother himself with listening. "Don't be stubborn", open the door, Sara said. It was useless; John didn't even make the slightest noise. After calling a few times, Sara lost her patience and she left him alone and rushed to Max. Maybe her husband would be able to do something, but before everything Sara explained the problem to Max.

That was the beginning of a dark phase between Max and John. Sara finally got successful in darkening the situation. Max raised his voice by John's room and called to him angrily. John who could hear well didn't expect to receive such a tone of voice from his dad. That's why he got a little scared. At first, he didn't react at all, but after a few times that his dad called, he opened the door cautiously. Max slammed the door backwards as soon as John opened the door and the door hit John's nose very badly. In fact, it caused his nose to bleed. John's nose hurt so badly, and he covered his nose with his right hand. Sara who was witnessing the situation got very happy and excited inside but she was smart enough not to show it on the outside. As a matter of fact, she showed a very sympathetic face. "Why didn't you open the door sweetie?" She asked John, pretending to be nice. Max's face had already turned ridiculously red. "Tell me now, did you touch the phone?" Max asked hastily. John who was still covering his nose just figured out what disaster had happened. What was the use though, he couldn't talk and it was already too late to solve the problem. In that situation Sara acted like a professional actress and she held her husband by his arms, preventing him from worsening the situation. John mumbled some stuff as usual, but not even a single word could be understood. It was about 10:00 p.m. Sara told Max about the time and that it was getting late. She was trying to encourage her husband to stop, like a mediator. "It's getting late honey. He has made a mistake and he is going to promise not to do it anymore", Sara said. "Now let's go to sleep", Sara continued pulling her husband's arm. Although she did have a hard time doing so, since Max was a very strong man. Finally, she succeeded and they both left John alone.

Poor John was very scared by then; so scared that he slammed the door to his dad and stepmom. His dad and stepmom were on their way to their bedroom when they heard the loud noise. All of a sudden Max tried to go back. "I should give him a good lesson", Max said. Sara prevented him. "Our five-year-old kid is getting very rude and out of control", Max said. "Just leave him alone, your health is more important. He has learned his lesson anyways", Sara said. Finally, Sara took him to bed and they turned off the lights.

The one who didn't turn off the light was John, who was still shaking due to extreme madness. They say don't make kids mad. They can do a lot of things such as committing suicide or harming others. They may get depression which is one of the worst scenarios. The light was still on in John's room, it was like he couldn't sleep. His eyes were teary and his body was still shaking. The person who didn't care at all was Sara. So many thoughts passed through John's mind such as praying. All of a sudden he thought maybe the doll was the cause of all the problems he had. Then he thought, that can't be and he remembered how much his mom loved him. His heart was full of sorrow anyways. On one hand, he thought the doll was troublesome and on the other hand he thought praying might solve his problems. He was getting confused and he didn't really know what to do. Sometimes he could picture his stepmom in the doll, why? Because stepmom wanted the doll too. John wanted to be the only one who loves the doll.

As a matter of fact, the doll belonged to him, not his stepmom. Stepmom could bring all the excuses in the world that the doll belonged to her, but it really didn't. John was getting crazy because of too many thoughts in his mind. All of a sudden he made up his mind and he ignored everything else, such as the bicycle and even his real mom. Yes, he had already made up his mind. Right or wrong didn't matter; nobody could change his mind. That night he started praying, nobody knew what he prayed for. Of course he couldn't talk but he mumbled some things as usual.

The next day when John woke up he noticed his doll's dress had changed. Who did that? He asked himself. Then he remembered what his stepmom had told him long time ago. How could she have come in my room last night, since my door was locked? John thought to himself. It's a nice dress anyways; maybe my stepmom has my room key. Oh yeah maybe it was really her who changed the dress. Who knows, John thought to himself, but he had already made up his mind. All of a sudden, he remembered one of Sara's dresses, which had the same pictures as his doll. Oh yes it is exactly the same. The pictures of red roses with red ribbons on the doll's skirt matched his stepmom's dress. Then he remembered that his stepmom told him about the fabrics he already had. So what is so strange about it? John asked himself. Anyways John wanted to put an end to his problems, that's why he didn't want to change his mind.

It was around 10:00 in the morning. John asked for his stepmom's permission to go outside for refreshment. Sara said, "Just be careful and come back as soon as possible." "I promise", John said and he ran to his room and took the doll with him. The stepmom had almost forgotten about the doll. John headed towards a huge bridge, which was about a quarter of a mile away from their house. He walked so fast that soon he got out of breath, but in the meanwhile he was very careful, so nobody could see him. Any witnesses could cause a lot of trouble and John knew it for sure. By the time he got under the bridge he was breathing very fast and loudly. He tried to focus on what he was going to do. First, he took a quick and careful look around. After, he made sure that there was nobody around. He started to mutilate his doll's body parts. He started with the right arm, then the left one. He did all that with so much anger, and then he threw the body parts far away apart from each other, under the bridge. Then he rushed back home.

Max was planning to leave the following day. The night before Sara and Max went to bed early and so did John. It was around 2:30 after midnight when everybody was sleeping. Sara started to mumble some words while she was asleep. That ended up waking up Max. Max thought that she was having a nightmare. Anyways Max couldn't wake her up. Then he tried to understand what Sara was mumbling. It was something starting with zo, zo, zo, Sara kept repeating. Max decided to shake his wife again but it was totally useless. Sara mumbled some stuff several times and then nothing else could be heard.

In the morning Max woke up to get ready for his trip, but to his surprise he found the space next to him empty. His wife wasn't there. At first he ignored it and he rubbed his head a little bit. All of a sudden he thought about last night, but he couldn't make any sense of it. I guess she was having a nightmare last night, Max thought to himself. Where is she now though? Max asked himself. Since he couldn't come up to any conclusion, he decided to quit thinking about it. She must be somewhere around, Max told himself and he got ready to dress up for his trip. John was still sleeping when Max left the house. Max just gave him a kiss before leaving. John was alone by himself since Sara was nowhere to be found.

Around 11:00 a.m., somebody called. John was awake by then, but he wasn't sure if he was allowed to grab the phone, especially after the incident. After a few times ringing somebody left a message. "This is detective Rogers with the police department. I was going to speak to Mr. Max Randall. Would you please give me a call back as soon as possible, thank you", the message said. John listened to the message but he didn't know what to do.

Soon the police called his dad's cell phone and they wanted him at the police department. Max went to the local police department. "May I talk to detective Rogers?" Max said. They led him to the detective's office. "Hi, how are you doing Mr. Randall?" "I'm doing fine and you?" Max responded. "I'm doing well, thank you", the detective said. "I was going to talk to you about your wife; when was the last time you saw her?" The detective asked. "I was with her last night but I didn't see her in the morning when I woke up", Max replied. "But you were together last night?" The detective asked. "Yes like I said", she was with me then, Max answered. "I'm sorry to inform you that your wife has been murdered", the detective said. Max was in shock and soon after, drops of tears appeared in the corners of Max's eyes. "No, that can't be", Max said. "She was my love, she was my hope, and she was my everything." "Somebody reported about the mutilated body parts to the police station, and we found blood everywhere around the body parts." Max was shocked, he couldn't believe his ears. "There is one thing that I was going to show you", the detective said. "It's a folded paper we found in your wife's pocket. We checked the pattern of hand writing; it doesn't belong to your wife", the detective continued. "May I see it?"

Max asked. "Sure, here you are", the detective said and handed the paper to Max. Max unfolded the paper very carefully and then he got shocked when he read what was on the paper. It read, "I love you." "Well there's nothing strange about it. She always loved her family", Max said. "Oh that's a great thing to hear, but like I told you the handwriting is not your wife's", the detective said. "Whose is it then?" Max asked. "Not quite sure yet, but most probably it belongs to your ex-wife", the detective said. "That can't be. Everything seems to be a mistake", Max said. "Well here we work by proofs and evidences. There is a slight chance of making mistakes that way." Max wanted to cry but he couldn't; it was too hard for him to carry such a burden of sorrow. He didn't even know what to say. "Well we are going to let you know about the pattern of writing as soon as we are sure about it", the detective said. "If you have any more questions feel free to call the number on the card", and the detective handed the card to Max. Max tried so hard to say thank you but he couldn't and he stepped out of the building.

Although he was very busy; he decided firmly to visit his ex-wife. Max didn't say anything to John about what had happened. "We have to pack up and visit your mom", Max told John. "You are an angel, like Sara, did you know that?" Max asked John. John listened but he couldn't talk. "By the way I was going to show you something", Max said. Then he pulled out a folded paper and then he unfolded it and showed it to John. John read the writing, but he couldn't talk. Now let's get ready to visit your mom, Max continued. Max's soul had been captured by Sara, how about his ex-wife. Did she get deleted from his memory? What about the blood connection between John and his real mother, Mary. Of course Max was trying to deny that, but is it really possible to deny a fact? Is it possible to deny the love between a mother and her child? What was Max trying to prove? Was he trying to mix up his life story with other important things? John was not aware of it.

Anyways they packed up for the trip. Mary was living very far from them. When Max and John arrived Mary's husband informed them of the hospital Mary was at. Mary had blood cancer and she was living her last days of her life. When they got to the hospital they found Mary on a bed in a very sad and bad condition. They had to nebulize her with morphine (a powerful drug used for reducing pain). At first John couldn't recognize his mom's face since she had no hair. Max told John she is your real mom. "How is everything?" Max asked his ex-wife. Mary was staring at Max as if she was looking at the middle of nowhere. "I brought your son with me, so you can see him again." At this time Max provided some room for John to get close to the bed. As soon as Mary saw his son, a smile appeared on her face. Mothers never forget their children. In the meanwhile, Max showed the paper to Mary. "Did you write this?" Max asked. As soon as Mary saw the note she went unconscious before being able to say anything. The next day Mary passed away and her note was the only thing left behind, from her to John.

www.ingramcontent.com/pod-product-compliance
Lightning Source LLC
LaVergne TN
LVHW020429080526
838202LV00055B/5095